Fingertips

by David Gallash
illustrated by Lee Anne Levin

Harcourt

Orlando   Boston   Dallas   Chicago   San Diego

Visit *The Learning Site!*
www.harcourtschool.com

Shut Out

Soccer practice had gone on longer than usual, and Louis was late for the meeting. All the older kids—eighth graders—on the staff of the *Messenger* were already there—Cheryl, Seth, Shelby, and Mark. Especially Mark.

"So," Mark was saying, "you all have your assignments. We'll be running a big ad for Bramson's Sport Shop, so we need to have the issue out by December 1. If anyone can't get copy to me by the Monday after Thanksgiving, you'd better let me know now."

Louis tried to slip into the room, but Mark turned at the sound of his footsteps. The other staff members saw him and nodded or smiled. They were always friendlier to him than Mark was.

"Oh, there you are, Stein," Mark said. "Glad you showed up. I need to talk to you about that interview you did with Coach Fuller."

Louis's cheeks burned. *Glad you showed up.* As if he ever missed a meeting! Usually he came early, hoping Mark would give him a choice assignment. It looked like he missed his chance today.

The other staff members began to leave.

Louis watched Mark tap his stylus on the braille board. Every time the stylus touched the page, it made a tiny hole. Louis knew the holes were in certain patterns. There was a different pattern of holes for each letter of the alphabet. Each number had its own pattern, too.

Louis wondered how Mark could make those holes with any precision when he never seemed to stop talking. Still, when Mark transcribed his braille into the computer, it always came out right.

Louis wondered about that, too. How did Mark know which computer keys were which? But that was a problem for another day. Right now, he wanted an assignment.

Sorry," Mark told him. "I already gave out everything. Maybe you'll get an assignment for the next issue." He spread the printed sheets on the table. "I had to change your basketball piece," he said. He ran his fingertips over his copy of what Louis had written. "Here we are. When did you talk to Coach Fuller?"

"I don't know. Last Tuesday, I guess," Louis said.

"Before Bruce Dowling got injured?"

"I guess so. He didn't say anything about Dowling being injured."

"When there are new developments on a story, you should always follow up on them," Mark said. "Everything the coach said about this new offense he's devised around Dowling will have to be changed now."

Later that afternoon, Louis told his mother about the problems he was having with the school paper.

"I don't need this," he told her. "I'm going to quit the paper. It's hard enough keeping up with schoolwork and soccer. I don't need to get put down by Mark Brovar. All the good story assignments go to the boarding students, not to day students like me. The boarding students live in the dormitory—and they're Mark's friends."

"Aren't they all older kids, too?" his mother asked.

"Well, yes, but why can't he give a seventh grader a chance? He never lets me show what I can do!"

"Louis, you knew things would be tougher at George Academy," his mother said. "You worked hard to get that scholarship. If being a star is so important to you, there are plenty of other schools around."

"That's not fair, Mom," Louis said.

"How long have you been at the Academy?"

"You know how long."

"Three months, and that's not very long. You're making good grades, and you're making friends. You'll prove yourself there. I know you will. Just accept that it's going to happen gradually."

Louis hoped his mother was right. Sometimes he felt as if he would never fit in at his new school.

The Storm

Thanksgiving Day was cloudy and cold. On Friday snow began to fall. By Saturday the wind had whipped it into a blizzard. The weather people called it the worst November storm in the city's history.

By Sunday morning 20 inches of snow had fallen, and electric power was out across a wide area.

The phone call came just after noon.

"Stein, am I glad I caught you!" said a familiar voice.

"Brovar?" said Louis.

"Right," said Mark. "Listen, I need a tremendous favor. Could you print out and edit my rough draft of my interview with the principal about the school dress code? It's on my computer at the dormitory."

"Sure," Louis began, "but—"

"That's great!" said Mark. "The file name for it is *messenger12.1.* I'm glad I could find a day student to do this. The airport is closed because of the storm, so I can't get back to school. I don't know when the airport is going to reopen, and I need—"

"Uh, Mark?" said Louis.

"What?"

"Do you have a hard copy anywhere? The power is out here. I can't open your file or run your printer."

There was silence on the phone.

"Brovar? Are you still there?"

"Yes," Mark said slowly. "Yes, there's a hard copy on my desk, but it's not transcribed. It's in braille. Do you think you can read it?"

Louis gave the matter a few moments' thought.

"Well, I can try," he said.

The buses weren't running. Louis pushed his way through the drifted snow to George Academy.

In Mark's dormitory room, Louis found the pile of paper with the raised dots. Beside it was Mark's stylus. He saw that Mark's computer had braille dots on all the keys. That was how Mark knew which key was which!

A braille printer was on a shelf next to Mark's standard printer. Someone has obviously devised a program to print files in braille, Louis thought. He'd have to ask Mark to show him how it worked.

Breaking the Code

Louis found a chart showing the braille alphabet. In the fourth grade he had been fascinated with secret codes. That made this job a little easier.

If Brovar had left a copy on a floppy disk, Louis thought, I wouldn't have to do this. I could have run the laptop on batteries and edited this. I've got to talk to him about that, too.

The electric power was still out that evening, so Louis had to work by candlelight.

He checked every word for the sake of precision. Gradually, he became familiar with the patterns of dots. Each pattern had from one to six dots. He just had to remember which pattern represented each letter—or number.

Mark had also used braille codes to punctuate the article. Louis figured out that an extra dot before a letter meant that it was a capital.

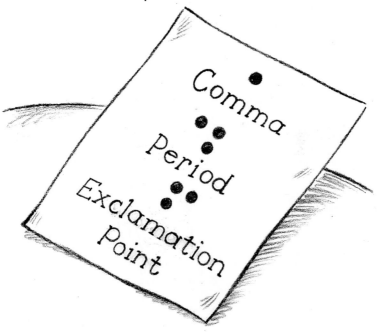

It was slow going at first, but after a while Louis began to feel as though he were reading with his fingertips. He tried it with his eyes closed but gave up quickly. He could feel the dots all right, but it took him too long to figure out each pattern.

It's a lot harder than it looks, he thought. I bet Mark had to practice a long time to get good at it.

Louis worked late into the night, but his mother didn't tell him to go to bed. They both knew there would be no school the next day.

"The *Messenger's* here!" students called across the snow-covered lawn. The snow had been shoveled off the sidewalks and now made huge piles.

It was December 1. Most of the newspaper staff had returned to school a day or two late, but the paper was out on time.

"You changed parts of my interview with the principal!" Mark said to Louis, but he was smiling.

"Well, you said the draft was rough," Louis said. He was smiling, too. "It was actually pretty good—but I made it even better!"

"And you read my braille, too," said Mark, still grinning. "Good work, Stein!"

The newspaper staff met later that day to begin planning the next issue. For a while, they talked about possible stories to include.

Then Mark said to the other staff members, "You know, I think Stein has earned himself a place on the first team. What do you think?"

They all began to talk at once, but they clearly agreed with Mark.

Mark turned to Louis, "Well, Stein, we usually don't give seventh graders jobs like this, but here's what I'd like you to do for the next issue…"

Louis just sat there with a silly grin on his face. He was on the first team! He was going to fit in at George Academy after all!